THANKSGIVING, HERE I COME!

For Nily, who carries on the sparkle of her mother's Thanksgiving table—DJS

GROSSET & DUNLAP
An Imprint of Penguin Random House LLC, New York

Text Copyright © 2020 by David Steinberg. Illustrations copyright © 2020 by Sara Palacios. All rights reserved. Published by Grosset & Dunlap, an imprint of Penguin Random House LLC, New York. GROSSET & DUNLAP is a registered trademark of Penguin Random House LLC. Manufactured in China.

Visit us online at www.penguinrandomhouse.com.

Library of Congress Control Number: 2019054589

ISBN 9780593094228   10 9 8 7 6 5 4 3 2 1

THANKSGIVING,
HERE I COME!

BY D. J. STEINBERG

ILLUSTRATED BY SARA PALACIOS

GROSSET & DUNLAP

THE BIGGEST TURKEY IN THE WORLD

Here comes a giant turkey
in the holiday parade.
It's bigger than a house—why is nobody afraid?
Me, I can't help thinking—
what if things go wrong?

That turkey could get loose like Godzilla or King Kong!
Can you just imagine?
It sure would be a pity . . .

if that turkey started stomping down the streets of New York City,
going "GOBBLE-GOBBLE-ROAR!"
while gobbling up the town . . .
Oh, *please*! Pray they were careful when they tied that turkey down!

I AM GRATEFUL FOR . . .

My teacher asks what I'm thankful for,
and I hope this won't sound jerky,
but one thing I am grateful for
is that I'm *me* and not the turkey.

9

ROCK STAR

I'm the star of the play.
Look at me—center stage—
when the *Mayflower* comes to dock.
I just hold my breath
and stand real still
'cause I play Plymouth Rock.*

(*Plymouth Rock—that's the real-life name of the rock
where the ship full of Pilgrims first came to dock!)

TURKEY HANDS

Everybody, trace your hands
for our handmade WELCOME sign!
We turn them into turkeys,
all standing in a line.
Ta-da! It's a turkey family
outside a turkey house.
And our puppy made a paw print, too—
voilà!—a turkey mouse!

THANKSGIVING GIVING

My family helps other people
who don't have enough to eat.
We go volunteer
this time every year
at a food pantry down the street.

We're all given jobs in the kitchen.
It's hard work preparing the meals.
But it's all worth our while
to see the guests smile—
I can't tell you how awesome that feels!

NANA'S SECRET HELPER

I'm Nana's Secret-Stuffing-Super-Helper—that is me!
I'm the secret to her Secret Stuffing Recipe, you see,
'cause after Nana makes it, she needs *me* to take a bite
and make absolutely certain that the stuffing came out right!

14

COUSINS BY THE DOZENS

I've got so many cousins,
I mix up all their names.
I *think* that one's Marissa.
That one there may be a James.

One's standing on my bookshelf.
One is screaming off his head.
One is banging on my drum set.
Two are jumping on my bed.
I want to tell my parents
that the cousins have to go,
but I know that they're our *guests*
so the answer will be *no*.

Guess I'd better find a way
to entertain these girls and boys . . .
I know! I'll go and pull out
my old favorite chest of toys.
The kids all dive into my stuff,
and I don't even mind, almost—
after all, they are my Cousin Guests
and I'm their Cousin Host!

WHEN DO WE EAT?!

The turkey is steaming.
The table is set.
How much more ready
can this dinner get?
Hurry up, people—
stop gabbing and greeting.
My stomach is rumbling . . .
Let's go do some *eating*!

MARSHMALLOW THIEF!

There must be a thief on the loose in our house.
Somebody call a cop!
Who left all the yams on the platter
but swiped the whole marshmallow top?!

TWO MILLION DISHES

Uncle Murray
doesn't eat gluten.

Aunt Amy eats no meat.

Which is why there's tofu turkey
with stuffing that's made without wheat.

Cousin Dahlia eats no dairy—
so there's macaroni that doesn't have cheese.

There are three different kinds of casseroles
'cause of everyone's food allergies.
For this one no sugar, for that one no nuts—
it gets complicated, you see.

Which is why it takes *two million* dishes
to feed our *one* family!

GRANDPA'S FAULT

I was drinking my sparkling cider
when Grandpa cracked a joke,
which made me laugh so hard,
it made me start to choke.
I *still* could not stop laughing—
it's *his* fault, I suppose,
that all that cider fizzled up
and bubbled out my nose!

WISHING ON A WISHBONE

It's no fair—*I* found the wishbone,
but we broke it and Arthur won!
So my brother gets all *his* wishes
while I get zilch, nada, *none!*

But just now he told me a secret.
Arthur wished for *my* wishes, too.
So although he got the bigger half,
our wishes will now *both* come true!

ONE MORE GUEST

There's one more guest for dinner.
While the people are eating theirs,
Oscar is having a feast of his own
underneath the chairs!

SCIENTIFIC DESSERT FACT

When you've gobbled up too much turkey
and stuffed your face till you hurt,
no matter how full you *thought* you were,
there is *always* room for dessert!

SO MANY PIES

Strawberry Rhubarb, Lemon Chiffon,
Key Lime and Pumpkin and Chocolate-Pecan.
So many flavors of pies you can try . . .
But me, I'll stand right here—you wanna know why?
I'm more of a Chocolate-Chip-Cookie-Type Guy!

FOOTBALL FEVER

A funny thing happens to Dad—
he's usually really tame—
but then—*CLICK!*—he starts yelling and jumping and shouting
as soon as he turns on the game!

WACKY FRIDAY

Our parents are up way too early.
They're dragging us out of our beds.
"Come on, we need to go buy *stuff*.
Wake up, you sleepyheads!"
Next thing I know, we're out driving
and we stop at each store without fail,
to fill up the car with *stuff* and *more stuff*
'cause today all that *stuff* is on sale!

Meadowview Mall

BOOKS ARE US!

THE CANDY EMPORIUM

THE SHOE BOUTIQUE

TED'S TOOLS & GADGETS

FRANK'S FURNITURE

TURKEY AGAIN?

Thanksgiving is over, but the turkey lives on.
We eat it all week 'cause we gotta.
It may show back up as a turkey potpie
or a turkey-cheese enchilada.
Oh, look—turkey chili with turkey soup . . .
How 'bout some *you-know-what* quiche?
Turkey stir-fry or a turkey-on-rye.
Turkey breakfast burritos? *Yeeeesh!*
Please, help! I'm totally turkeyed out
with leftovers up to *here*.
I'll be fine if I don't see a turkey again,
at least till Thanksgiving next year!